U.S.S

U.S.S

Unidentified School Students

Jodi Dulecki

author**HOUSE**®

AuthorHouse™
1663 Liberty Drive
Bloomington, IN 47403
www.authorhouse.com
Phone: 1-800-839-8640

First published by AuthorHouse   08/05/2011

ISBN: 978-1-4634-3841-8 (sc)
ISBN: 978-1-4634-3840-1 (ebk)

Library of Congress Control Number: 2011912758

Printed in the United States of America

Any people depicted in stock imagery provided by Thinkstock are models, and such images are being used for illustrative purposes only.
Certain stock imagery © Thinkstock.

This book is printed on acid-free paper.

Because of the dynamic nature of the Internet, any web addresses or links contained in this book may have changed since publication and may no longer be valid. The views expressed in this work are solely those of the author and do not necessarily reflect the views of the publisher, and the publisher hereby disclaims any responsibility for them.

Dedication

I would like to dedicate this to all of my friends, they have helped my through this all. There are too many to name but the ones that do know, you guys rock! I would also like to dedicate this book to my parents for helping me write. Encouraging me to keep writing, no matter what happened.

Elana

I was starting to walk to the bus stop as I waited for Jason to come; he was usually there first in the morning. But he never came, so I just sat by myself listening to everyone talking. I could hear little snips of every conversation. The football players, for instance, talked about the game and what should have happened like so: "Did you see me running down the field? That was a total foul . . ."

I rolled my eyes as they would go on and on about it. Then Erik my clothes designer and one of my closest friends sat next to me his dirty blond hair was cropped short and his eyes were like emeralds. But the only thing that set him apart from any other person is his height and clothes. I mean the guy could do wonders for other people but for him that's another story today he was wearing neon, green pants, neon red tee shirt, and a neon yellow vest but he was still a fun guy. "Hi." I said as he sat down next to me, "Hey, your eyes look as stunning as ever."

He said as, he was eyeing my lacey lilac long sleeve shirt. Oh, by the way my eyes are a wonderful lilac so it's a good thing for my eyes to 'glow' with the shirt. I smiled and blushed; we talked the whole time, when we got off we ran (mainly me) into Scarlet who thought in her own world she ruled the school but she was a totally prissy and had her own little poesy that did everything that she told them to do. Her curly chocolate brown hair was just supermodel approved, as it always was, and I could feel her blue-brown eyes boring into my own. Her full lips were a shining scarlet she was wearing a way too short red plaid skirt also a knitted red turtleneck sweater "Hey red, nice outfit who picked it out for you your mom?"

She asked and her poesy snickered like there was no tomorrow. I sighed and looked down at my elbow length blood red hair but it was so silky and colorful I don't think anyone has more colorful hair then I but, did use that sigh for my nickname 'hi red' 'what's up red?' Well it just stuck so it no longer is an insult. I smiled deviously and had a good come back for her "Thanks so much Scarlet. Now were you going?"

I took a pause and circled her and asked, "A strip club?"

Surprised at how I could humor myself but all the bystanders that wanted to see a catfight could get to see one Scarlet was not a happy girl then I turned around and said, "Could I have silence?"

After I asked that everyone shut it as soon as I spoke, and I mean that it was a first that anyone would listen to me so I was shocked as it was so I started with a calm tone then it got stronger when I got to the end, "well this is your life but still do you want to listen to everything that Scarlet says? I don't know about you but I vote not who wants to stand up for themselves? Scarlet isn't the boss, she can't make you do anything. This is our school as much as her own. Why does she get to have more of a say then the rest of us?"

There was a light mummer running threw the crowd then I could hear someone coming and shut up immediately.

I couldn't believe who it was, Mrs. Higgans the cruelest teacher in Husky High but, she did have a soft spot for Scarlet this is the reason that I get so many detentions but anyway, she has spiky gray hair and dead looking brown eyes. She looked around and asked, "What are all of you looking at?"

She posed the question as if it was for the prissy pants herself, Scarlet here we go again (I rolled my eyes). She cleared her throat and started her lie like this: "Well first Elana walked off the bus and purposely ran into me and I said 'hi Red, I love your outfit.' Then she asked me 'hey Scarlet, where are you going to the strip club?' After that Erik started cracking up. So I whispered to my friend that we weren't going to let Elana rule the school any more."

That was a total lie 'cause I don't even like to speak in my classes so I don't think that is even possible but she could pull it off. "Then everyone started to agree,"

She took a dramatic pause, "but then she told them that she could give them everything that they wanted."

Another total lie, my parents' barley have enough money to keep a roof over my head and food on my table. "Then you came along so that no one could say any more things about me that make me feel bad."

She concluded triumphantly, she won I couldn't compete with that then Mrs. Higgans smiled warmly at Scarlet then gave me the cold shoulder, and asked, "Do you think that it is true or false?"

She asked knowing that I would say false so I thought about it and said in a voice smaller then a whisper "false."

She sighed and made the tisk, tisk, tisk sound when she said "the word of someone who speaks a lie."

Gave me a detention slip my parents had to sign it. "Oh great."

I muttered to myself it was my second one this week my parents are going to kill me! The first bell rang as I trudged on to my next class. Math when I walked in I saw Jason tutoring

Mr. Gringer, well let me paint a picture of what Jason looks like. He has black hair and chocolate brown eyes that you could just sink into and forget the rest of the world around you with sleek black glasses he was the cutest boy in school the other thing that had girls busting down his doors was that he is the smartest boy in the school, but anyway Mr. Gringer is no push over he has brown-blond hair and blue-green eyes that were glued to the paper as Jason was showing him how to do it. Well I sat down and waited for the second bell to ring and everyone to pile in and when they saw Jason half the girls swooned and the boys became overly jealous and I thought *Oh great, here we go again.* Then class started. As he called attendance, it was peaceful alone time for me.

Jason

"No, no."

Then I pointed to the spot where he messed up he looked at the paper as if it were a bomb and he had to defuse it within twenty seconds. I looked at the clock and saw that the bell was going to ring within five, "Ok I've got to go but I'll come back at lunch and help you with the problems."

All the girls swooned as I left, class started in five, four, three, two, one. (I was in my seat by two.) Then the twelfth grade math teacher came and taught us about the equation of pie ad how we can get the square root of it. I already knew this so all I did was use my laptop and look up things so I could see what the textbooks say and if they were wrong. Thirty minutes later, the bell was about to ring so I got packed. Then I went to Social Studies one of the three classes that I had with Elana. She was the sweetest thing you'll ever meet she is so down to earth I cant think of any other words to describe her with so I think I'll just show you. I walked into Socal.S and saw that she was already there but

I just took my normal seat next to her while I looked at her she was watching the clock. As her blood red hair swooped while she looked back to the teacher and back to the clock. Her lilac eyes darting everywhere she looked. Then she whispered, "Did you get everything that you needed for our project?"

I smiled "Down packed."

Then our teacher walked in and the class started and the day blurred together Science, Socal.S, Trig., Government, and Band. These are the classes that I have that I have with Elana Socal.S, Trig, and band. Band was the only time that I had to slow down and just relax. I play the French horn and Elana plays the Tenor saxophone she has the greatest sound out of all the others and there are seven to be exact. But I bet she could even out do a pro.

At the end of the day we rode the bus together so we talked to each other for the whole ride and when we got back she asked of she could come over 'cause her parents weren't home from there work and she needed me to give her a drive to were she is going to see if she could get a job so she could give her parents what she made on a daily basis was around five dollars an hour and she worked for five hours so maybe on a good day twenty-five on a bad day she would get around maybe twenty dollars tops. But we started to work on our project when my mom walked in so we had to hide everything his mom was an artist so she would make us add a touch of color to it so we just found something that we could be doing so we started to quiz each other on our trig vocab so his mom could see that we were doing something related to school. Then later before she had to go to her job offer we watched *Land of the lost* my parents watched with us and asked what was the scientific value of this movie we looked at each other and I said "Our science teacher wants us to find a movie that we like and try to find the scientific value of it and this is . . ."

Elana cut me off (she always caught me when I fumbled). "Well the scientific value is that it can show us that there are possibilities outside out normal box that we like to stay inside."

Then it was five she had to go to her job offer we drove her there and then she told us that her parents knew where to pick her up so we left. Then when I got home I fell asleep.

General Peaters

"Um, sir?"

The colonel asked as I walked on to area 51's dry desert he was out of breath trying to catch up to me. "What do you want Colonel?"

I asked he sounded scared like someone got in and took a dozen pictures of the aliens we have captive. "Sir, someone hacked into out system and copied all of our information about everything that happened even the pictures that we took of the aliens."

I froze in place this was the worse news he could have given me. "Where did this come from?"

"Were already on it sir it ended up showing up at Husky High in Nevada its vary close here."

We were in my office when he finished I picked up the phone and dialed "GAF I need you ASAP."

We got everyone that matters onto the helicopter even the best interrogator that I know Agent Adoms. While we flew I looked over the files of every kid in that school; but these five kids caught my eye . . . These are the files I showed to Agent Adoms. He looked them over and circled them in red pen, mixed them in with the rest of the school. He was going to show them that they are the ones that we are looking at. But like all of the schools do they say they will be asking every one questions. I've gone to more then enough schools to know that.

Jason

I forgot to tourer Mr. Gringer yesterday. So I
decided to go to school earlier then I normally
would. When I show up I knock on his door,
it takes him a few minutes to answer. I hear
drawers closing with a loud thud, papers being
sifted through, and typing on the key board.
Nothing out of the ordinary, nothing until I heard
static coming from behind the locked door. I
some how remember how Elana used a bobby
pin in something like this situation. Lets just
say that she locked herself out of her room. I try
it and it fails. How can someone do this without
trying it a few times?! I yell at myself. When she
showed me this I was about eight and she was
maybe seven or eight. I knew this for a fact that
she had never done it before. But now wasn't the
time to get mad and just quit. I needed to get in
there and see what was going on. But that was
the difficult part. Getting in. How I didn't know
but I was going to no matter how long it took me
to devise a plan to get in the class room. I look
at the door and the knob turns ever so slowly,
Mr. Gringer peeks out slightly then invites me

in. After five minutes of I asked, "what was that static sound that I heard when I was outside the door?" there was some hesitance in his voice when he asked me with an uncertain cough "Um, do you know Elana well?" My eyes widened, "So you are..." He nodded and I was struggling for words. I was walking to my locker my mouth gaping. It was time for school to start. I get my stuff and I'm off to my Home Room. Home Room was just around the corner and I was almost there with my slip, saying that I was helping a teacher. I slip in the class room without being noticed. Hand the note to my teacher sit back and wait for the first bell to ring.

Zach

I sit down in math and I see Erik he was the laughing stalk of the school but since that new kid what was her name Deanna or something like that everyone left him alone. The Algebra teacher walked in and she stopped and saw that there was some thing written on the white board: *What is the square root of math?* Then it had a stick person farting I smiled and as the teacher walked out and everyone started laughing except Deanna or what ever her name is. I walked over to her and whispered "why aren't you laughing? What is your name?"

"I'm Elana and I just don't think that it's that funny."

My mouth was gaping "What that's comedy gold there."

Then everyone started asking the all-star question 'who did it?' Then I raced back to my desk and stood on it and said "I did it, it took me five extra minuets in detention room, you were there weren't you, Elana?"

Getting detention was the only thing that made you a somebody and I knew that she wouldn't like the attention much, but I had to. She turned just as red as her hair. Then she stated this, "I have no clue what you are talking about."

She said, as her teeth were clenched. I laughed out loud "this is the goody two shoes? Or as I like to call her the detention regular."

That got everyone's attention and they all looked like they were going to start ganging up on her then they all sat back into their seats. The teacher looked around the class and asked the all star question "who did it?"

She said as the principal walked in with a detention slip Elana sank into her seat and waited for all eyes to go to me but they all looked at each other and then they all looked at her then she stood up and said what she'd wanted to say the moment she walked in "I didn't do it, it was Zach."

She said pointing an accusing finger at me I smiled devilishly then I looked at the principal and then to the teacher. "Yes, I did it but I didn't do it alone Elana did it with me," she was gawking at me "she watched me do this and didn't do anything to stop me . . ."

Then there was a crash everywhere then the principal went to see what it was that was making the sounds. Then we heard on the P.A. someone that we didn't want to hear.

Elana

There was a low gruff voice that came on and said, "This school is under lock down; there will be a guard at every door and we will ask everyone a few questions."

Then Mrs. Gardner started frantically telling us that we had to tell the truth. There was another deep voice outside the door and then some one with black-brown hair and wearing a or at least it seemed a vary expensive suit and black sunglasses that were meant to keep us from seeing his eyes, they didn't work that well if they hit the light just right you could see his almost black eyes. He looked at the piece of paper and said two names, "Zach and . . ."

He looked and then said "Elana, is that how you say it? Anyway you need to come with me."

I stood reluctantly and went with him and then Mrs. Gardner said as we left "tell the truth,"

We walked in the hall way and then Zach said with his green eyes were smiling and then he said, "What do you think that they want from us? Do they want us to do some undercover work . . ."
He went on and on and then I smacked him on

the back of the head and his brownish-blackish hair flew across his face, he said, "what am I Tony from N.C.I.S?"

I laughed we walked into the principals office.

We sat in the waiting room where I found Jason nervously chewing his thumbnail and sat by him, and whispered "why are we here?" He whispered back "I didn't get the project done, so that's why they are here I need to give it to them tomorrow."

Then I saw evil and darkness shadow the room it was the devils child herself Scarlet walked in and sat on the chair in the farthest corner and she did her make-up she did this twice, maybe three times a day four on a good day even more on a better day, but away from her I saw a red skyscraper and looked up "Erik what are you doing here?"

I asked everyone that I knew on a personal level was here, what was happening here? He responded with a shrug and sat next to me. They called me into the principals office and then I saw that they had sound proof glass to replace the school safe brand that had the wires were inside so I walked in causally as if this was nothing new. Then the guy who brought me there was sitting in the chair on the other side of the table there was one chair left so I just looked at it as if I didn't know what it was. He was as calm as though he was at house witch freaked me so I didn't sit I just stood there and asked in a strong but thoughtful tone "is there anything that you would like to go over if there isn't then I have no reason to be here."

He nodded to the chair so I sat but I perched at the edge of it. "I just have a few questions to ask you that's all." I smiled "so you're an interrogator?"

I asked with very fake but very believable excitement. He fought back "yes, is there a problem with that?"

I sighed and shook my head "I know all your tricks I love to watch real people get interrogated I've seen everything that there is to know about it so, lets just cut to the chase. My dad is an interrogator and he told me that if your eye starts twitching, like that,"

And I pointed to his eye as it twitched "that means that you want to know something and will do anything for it. You can't hold me here unless you're going to charge me with something, so charge me or I'll leave right now."

He heaved a sigh "ok, Ill charge you with fraud and hacking."

My mouth gaped open then I thought about what my dad told me to do in a situation like this. Nothing came to mind "I can't hack; I can't even work Face Book. And fraud what did I do that is considered fraud?"

I asked hopefully to find a loophole. He shook his head and said as if these were things that he said everyday. I think he did but anyway. "You did fraud by doing trickery and causing pain to someone the person who gave you the job, to be exact."

With that he was trying to butter me up so that cooking me would be a breeze but I was something that didn't want to be cooked. "Well how exactly did I 'cause pain to the person?'"

I put the air quotes over cause pain to the person? He knew what I was up to so he fired back "he told me that he didn't want to give you the job but he just said that you could have the job, now why would he do that?"

I stood up in my chair and shot back as soon as he was done "I did nothing that would have caused him harm! He's a liar! I didn't say anything besides 'can I have the job?' then I showed him what I could do with a spatula. And he was flabbergasted so he shook my hand and said 'you've got the job.' The End; case closed, or what ever you want to say."

I gave him a serous look and then he straitened the papers on the table and then said, "You're free to go."

As I left I saw that Erik was curled up in a corner and sobbing I walked over to the big guy and rubbed him back, he jumped at first then he hugged me and asked "what did he do to you in there we all saw you screaming at him then he put his hand up and you stopped right when he did that and I mean it was scary."

He wiped the last few tears out of his eyes and looked at me with a look that I've never seen him have all pure seriousness and asked, "What dose he want from us?"

I shrugged "he didn't tell me but he thought that I could hack into the computer."

We both laughed at the thought I could barley work anything on that stupid thing Erik was teaching me so I was getting better. Then they called Jason into the interrogation room.

Jason

"Jason we just need you to answer a few questions."

Then lead me into the room that they took Elana to. There was a guy sitting there and he gestured to the seat and I sat down and got comfy, the exact opposite of what Elana did. Then he started by what Elana said was the first thing that any interrogator would do soften you up by flattering you with things that were so true and you could lie, but it is vary difficult to do with a professional Elana said that they would stretch the truth. That is what I was afraid of; he could lie but make me think that he was telling the truth. I wiped the thought from my mind and just started to twiddle my thumbs then he started with the buttering up; another way that Elana explained it. "My name is agent Adoms, and I hear that you are the smartest person in this school, is that true?"

He asked and then whispered "you know that I think that your hiding something from the whole school, what do you think of that you tell me and I tell you what were here for."

I frowned he was good but not good enough "I don't have anything to hide form the area 51 agents."

I said as   simply as I could, his gaped open and was staring as if I were an alien. "How did you know that?"

I sighed, "Well I heard one of the guards were talking about aliens so that is what I thought that was what you were looking for,"

I shrugged and got to the point were he was going to blow up in my face then thought *what did Elana say to do in a situation like this?* Then a thought snapped into my head just listen to what he says then stand up and go for the door unless he charges me with something. "What do you do here? What are your talents . . ."

He rambled on then when he was done I stood up and walked to the door he looked as if he were daydreaming "where are you doing?"

I smiled "Leaving, or do you want to charge me with some thing?"

I asked challengingly he drew a deep breath he let it out slowly "alright you may go."

That was short I wonder . . .

Agent Adoms

Oh well their goes another one. I thought to myself this one was going to crack no matter what. I'm done with everyone knowing what interrogators do! From Elana because she knows all these people as friends or something closer . . . but what did I know about teenagers? "This one she is the popular one she'll be the one that Ill get something out of. Get her."

I told the girl who was going to get anyone that I sent her to get. She came back with a girl that looked just like a supermodel and with everything was perfect but not at all like Elana she was just all natural these kids could and possibly are rivals. She sat down and just looked in her make-up mirror and she just sat there like there was no one here with her. I stood up and stood behind her and asked "would you like something to drink?"

She gasped *how the heck can you sneak up on someone looking in a mirror?* "You scared me half-to-death!"

She almost yelled at me she cocked her head to the side then asked, "Where am I?"

My mouth was gaping when she asked that question. I took a deep breath and decided that she was going to be the easiest to crack she is dumber then well a blond, I said "you are here so I can ask you a few questions about Elana."

She seemed like she was about to burst-out laughing, "what's so funny?"

I asked in a serous tone that got her to shut up vary fast, then like I was stupid asked "didn't you see in that file you have about me that me and her are rivals and will forever will be?"

I close my eyes then rubbed them making sure that this wasn't a joke that I wasn't hallucinating. I think that my eyeballs were popping out of my head because she asked, "Dude? Hey, are you ok when can I get out of here?"

She waved her hand in front of my face. "Yea I'm ok, but how did you go from stupid to smart like that?"

I snapped my fingers to show her what I meant. She looked at me confused then smiled and answered "oh that, that's just play so that people will think that they can get things out of me easer."

I smiled, "well you sure fooled me."

This was going to be so easy to get things out of her know, I get her to like me then I just get answers out of her. "So what is it like ruling the school from a girl's point of view?"

She talked about how everyone did what ever she wanted him or her to do what ever she wanted him or her to do. She paused "what do you mean from a girls point of view?"

"I just thought that someone as smart as you would guess that I was just like you when I was on high school."

She smiled she knew what I was doing or did she . . . "Ok I get what your trying to get me to do, my parents own the school and I've seen them get interrogated your just trying to butter me up so I will roll over on command, I'm a dog that doesn't want to roll over. And I'm leaving unless your going to charge me with something, Peace out see you; never."

She stormed out of here like a tornado even taking the file I had on her. I smiled *she's good.* I looked at the second to last file that I had it was the kid neon sign Erik "send him in."

I said pointing to the picture. I waited a few minutes and looked over his file, he is the best basket ball player this school has ever had, he is vary creative, vary good clothes designer in the world but the only thing that he cant dress well is his own back. This was a comment from one of the teachers I was taken a back when I saw that he's had around 14 detentions this year all for keeping a secret for his friends. *This isn't going to be as easy as I thought.* Here he comes I look at about where every kid that comes in but for this one I have to look up which is odd because I am around five nine, but he was six feet two or just around that he was wearing red everything red pants red tee red sweat shirt it looked good but he was just a softie "Hey, I'm agent Adoms and your name is?"

He smiled shyly "I think that you should know everyone says that you have files on us and Scarlet showed us that you have files on us so I think you should know what my name is what I like to do, what sport I play, and what teachers think of me, that is why I think that you should know my name."

Man, this one will do anything to help his friends this is how he gets in trouble this school has low tolerance for this type of thing. "Ok I get it so I'm just going to ask you a few questions about Elana is that ok?" "No that's no ok I cant just talk about my friends behind there backs its just not that nice and neither are you so I'm going to leave unless your going to charge me with something, and yes Elana did teach me that."

He walked out of the   room as if he won a war. **THIS IS IT I CANT TAKE THIS NO ONE WILL TALK!** I have one more friend to talk to Zach. "Bring him in and with luck I will have something come out of him!"

I yelled at her she ran and got him but this took a while he was the class clown he tried to get out of it but Heather was going to get him in here one way or another. He comes in and

Heather for the first time locked the door I saw why Zach was throwing himself ageist the door trying to break it back open. *This one is a crack head.* "Ok Zach we get it the door is locked,"

He jumped I don't think that he saw me there "don't give yourself a concussion kid,"

He sat down breathing heavily "what do you want with me? I didn't steal something from the government."

He sounded like he was going to pass out "we don't think that you stole something from us although you did steal a lot of things in the mall the grocery store . . . where haven you stolen from yet?"

He had to think about that, "I don't think that there is a place in this town that I haven't stolen from if its new Ill get to it."

"Well son I think I can tell you were we're from."

I whispered this into his ear "We're from Area 51."

His mouth was big enough to catch a trout in "shut your mouth or Ill have to wipe your mind unless you tell me about the kid called Elana."

"To be as true as blue I don't know that much about her except that she comes to detention a lot I think that Scarlet gives her all of them, can I go?"

"Yea go on."

He came over and shook my hand and before I thought about it all the files were gone. I laughed he forgot to say 'yet'.

Elana

This is too much I can't even think what they may have said to all of my friends I just can't believe that agent Adoms fell for Zach's what happened I'm scared act, just so he could get our files mine had my name circled in red but so was Jason's. It said everything that the teachers know about me. But there was just one comment that I wanted to erase from agent Adoms file on me, 'is the bully to Scarlet Copper and I would highly recommend keeping them away from each other.' That was from Guess who Mrs. Higgans. I wanted so bad to see the sadness on her face when I kill Scarlet. But that was not what people wanted form the person that got these people to come here. My eyes started welling up and I started crying I had no clue why then I saw that every eye was on me as I had my break down I snapped my head up and looked around "what we won't get to see any of our parents little or big bros or sis. I just want to go home who else wants to go home we need to stick together and make sure that no one will get anything out of us. Deal? Who ever has a deal with me say, I."

Everyone said 'I' even Scarlet "why should I let you in on this all you ever do to me is bag on me and you . . . what are you doing?"

She sighed,

"I'm doing what's right. And if any of my friends ask you guys made me do it by saying that you would take away my make up. Got it?" "Yep," "so what's your plan?"

"Well we have to act like we never said any of this. We act like mortal Enemies or friends, all right we can't tell anyone but there are some things that you have to promise that you won't tell any one."

Then I whispered them the secret they all agreed that they would tell no one. What do you think that I could let you know? You're just a random person. "What do you want with me Scarlet?"

I whispered. "I just want you to know that I like you, your hair your smile everything about you, I know what am I getting to? I'm just jealous of you that's why I bag on you, so don't take it personally, K?"

My eyes widened as if they were about to fall out of their sockets. Then I whispered, "What I thought that you did that so you could . . . what are you saying?"

That was all that I could say in this moment of shock. She shook her head as if the answer was right in front of me . . . Right in front of me? Hmm, I looked up and I saw what she was talking about a mirror for the second time in my life I looked good in my own skin. Scarlet on the other hand looked like her skin was glued on and she didn't like it that way. But me I'm just comfortable in my own skin I was happy that she actually told me that she was jealous of me, this was great. But I wasn't going to tell any one this was something that I could use on her later. I went to sit next to Erik and Jason. They were both looking at the ground as if they were the boys that tried to ask Scarlet out but failed harshly. "What's wrong guys?"

I asked them but I was deep in though things that I thought of were clear I had to try and reason with them they have to let us see where they work so that we know who and what and why were talking to them. And we deserve to know what they want from us. "We need to know."

I said with out realizing it they all looked at me like I was saying something in a different language. "What?"

I asked as if I just didn't even know what I was saying myself. Jason answered, "I know we need to know. I may be able to make them what they want from us and give them what they want only if they show us what they are hiding from the world or what ever."

I had to think about it, "Zach are you good at lying and making it look like you may be on to something?"

Why did I even have to ask, he answered automatically, "yea, now this is going to sound weird coming from me but, what are you getting to?"

"We can take down his 'castle' brick by brick."

"Scarlet what are you good at?"

I asked looking down in the 'interrogation room' he was arguing with the lady who had to kill us if he told her to. "I can make anyone look like there an adult or pretty close to,"

"Good we can use that, Jason what can you do that can help?"

That took him a while to answer we all knew what his first answer would have been math but, I knew that he could do a lot more then he thought.

"I can know what people are feeling just by watching there facial expressions, like now Scarlet is trying to tell me to get on to the fact what I can do to help,"

he took a breather "well we have to make a hand signals so that we all know what they are feeling, but we cant under any circumstances can we use sign language. Is that clear?"

We all nodded, this was going to be a long night. It was just about time for bed when they came in with sleeping bags so we wouldn't run from this room they locked the door behind them. I sat strait up the rest were hesitant I sighed "guys they left and they are almost wait now they are in the teachers lounge, you know that its not fair that almost all the teacher got to go home and all us kids have to just sit here and wait."

I just thought for the next thirty minutes wile they were trying to pick the lock and let me tell you they were doing a pretty bad job at to. "Guys, I'll show you how to do it they seem to have left the key in the lock so we will be out."

I heard a satisfying *click, click, thump.* we were out there was no stopping us we were walking down the hall triumphantly until I heard footsteps on the right of me about a good three feet away but, we all could hear them they were wearing loud combat boots. I looked and saw that the bathrooms were not locked they were probably just for the kids to use if they had to go. The closest one was a girls' the boys were arguing that it wasn't fair that we had to go into the girls bathroom. "Get in there or well get caught and be sent to juvie. And we don't want to be around a lot a what ever are in there. And no I don't want to know."

We got them in there with a promise that this wouldn't leave this ladies room. We all paired up and got into a stall standing on the toilets so that there would be no feet underneath the stall to make them look. But they weren't one of those people that make sure that there is nothing in the stalls they just walked and walked out. "That was close."

I whispered then I heard a slight buzzing. Then I saw red lights I opened the door a crack and Erik said that they were lasers. "Erik I need to get up on your shoulders."

He nodded I felt like I was going to crash threw the ceiling then I looked up and saw that they were like the ones in the hall the square ones that if you push up they go up. So that is what I did and then I was in a dark place that seemed like it was covered in gross stuff that I couldn't figure out what it was. I crawled over to the one that I thought was the one above Scarlet and Jason and I guessed correctly I looked at the space and saw that they were holding each other scared I decided to make a little joke they were going to freak I crawled silently to the spot where I came in and whispered to Erik "act like your scared when I pull you up."

Then I made all the noise that I could without making it too loud. I could hear the gasps of everyone that didn't know about it. Then I grabbed Erik and hoisted him up he was heavy I whispered, "Can you try and lift your self?"

He did it and he looked like he was being dragged up there and then I grabbed Zach he screamed silently then he saw my face and he covered his mouth and snickered. He mouthed *'good joke Jason and Scarlet are just plain freaking out.'* Then I had to cover my mouth and then I went for Jason and he tried to get out and he didn't look at my face he just started slapping me and I held his hand and he looked and he laughed "one more to go."

I said to my self. I reached for Scarlet and she wasn't there. I heard her come up behind me. "What are you doing scaring everyone? You almost gave me a heart attack!"

"Well it seems like you were the only one that was scared of me they all burst out laughing when they saw that it was me, and Zach you thought that you were the king of pranks well look at the new queen."

We all laughed and we went on with what we were supposed to do. I heard a snore that sounded like a warthog. We all said at the same time "Earl."

He was the weirdest nerd in school and he was the only one that thought thick glasses and snorting was the coolest thing on the planet. We crawled out of the ceiling but, Erik had to go first and he was only inches away from the ground so he barely made a noise. He helped everyone out so that they barely heard us. Then we blockaded the doors, I whistled "everyone get up!"

All the heads popped up and they looked in our direction and they stood up reluctantly walked slower then a snail with a limp. "Guys do you want to get out of this school? Then let's show these people that kids don't want to be messed with!"

I yelled if they only could hear us know everyone answered "yea we don't want to be locked in this school,"

What I said next was surprising to all of us "we are going to show those adults that you cant mess with the kids with out getting the back talk of there life!"

I heard a choir of "yea!"

"Then we need a plan to take down these new comers by doing what we do best, BEING KIDS! What adults don't like are us! We give them their headaches, mood swings, and well all of the stress in their lives! Are you with me?!"

"YEA!"

"Well first we need a plan and that includes all of you we need clothes that will make us well some of us, anyway we need a few volunteers to act as adults one has already signed up, Zach I need you to get some more people who will help us with what we have to do."

He started to walk away I yelled, "Make sure that they are good liars like you."

I think that he blushed when I said that. "Scarlet, we need you and your posses help in the make up department, I can get you all into the drama class so that you can get all the stuff that you need K?"

"Alright, let me get them rounded up and well meet you . . ."

I had to think about that "where we got here make sure that they want to do this because that place that we came out of is full of stuff that I have no clue what is what. Just make sure that they know that they will be doing something that may just change their lives forever."

She gracefully walked away and found three of the five the others were talking to there boyfriends. She found them and told the same thing that I told her they all nodded enthusiastically, hey what can I tell you they all love doing make up. Any way kids were running around finding a job that suited them when they were all in there little groups I walked over to where Zach was he had a troop full of kids that said they are good liars. "Ok Zach I need you to ask them a question and you need to see if they are lying or not K?"

"Alright but you may want to watch this I will need you to tell me if they are what you wanted."

I sighed, "Alright what do we have here?"

"Here we go, ok first question when was you last detention?"

I looked at the boy and then I recognized him he was always in detention this ought to be good.

"Last month I was doodling in my note book and the teacher caught me so she said that I was supposed to be taking notes."

I looked at him, "was that a lie? You have to tell me the truth or I will kick you out of this squad got it?"

"Yes ma'am I was lying but I think that you fell for it."

I smiled working with the ninth graders was hard work "you would have fooled me except that I was in detention with you yesterday."

He had to look at me to figure out that I was the one that helped him with his trig. "Oh I know you I just didn't know that you were this out going."

I blushed this wasn't going the way that I thought. "This is going to be tough for you to we need you to act as my lawyer so that I will be able to fight this and well we'll need other people that are good at lying to help Jason, Zach I'm sorry that you can't be one of the kids who can help but they are interrogating you to. Also we need a girl who can lie for Scarlet so that the boy isn't drooling after her and we need a vary effective one for Erik he is going to be the toughest one to find a lawyer for, but this may end up in the history books,"

I smiled broadly this was going to end up in the history books I'm sure of that. I found the only lunch table that was still up, "guys we all love how enthusiastic you all are but this is our only chance . . . if we mess this up we have no were to turn, this is our time to show the adults that we are not that weak and just plain fools. WHAT ARE WE?"

I yelled to them "KIDS!"

There response was almost just immediate.

"WHAT ARE WE FIGHTING FOR?!"

"OUR SCHOOL, FRIENDS, AND OUR FREEDOM!"

"ALRIGHT LETS DO THIS THING!"

Only if my parents could see this it was the world war III. "Ok make up group lets go I'll be back pranksters we need you to make your school famous stink bombs, liars get in you places when we get back we need you to be ready for a make over!"

Lets go I thought to my self "Erik we need you."

He came over and helped me up and then I helped all the other girls up and we crawled to the to the drama department and took all of the things that the girls thought we would need. We got up there with the latter and I pushed the latter over so that it looked just like it did when we came here. When we got back I gave the girls the entire thing make up and stuff to make it look even more realistic. I walked to the pranksters and saw that they had like fifteen done that was a lot for about three minuets. But they were the real deal and then I looked to the Nerds and they were making a knock out spray that if we were to get caught then we could spray them with this and they would be knocked out and mind wiped they even got out all the kinks. This was going great, I walked over to the tech peps and they were making me a phone so that I could call my 'lawyer' I went to see how they were doing they were putting the stuff on that makes you face look vary different my lawyer and Scarlet's was finished and wow was she right they did look like they were adults. I grabbed them and took them to the lying chamber; it was basically where the lunch ladies' cooked. "I will be asking you questions that you may hear and well you know what to do."

I cleared my throat and I made sure that I sounded just like agent Adoms, "Ok thank you for coming and well I have a few questions for your client,"

They nodded solemnly "Scarlet what do you think of Elana? Ok now you have to act like she whispered what she wants to say so basically she will say 'make it sound like I said it' or things like that so what is you response?"

"My client would like me to state any and everything that she wants to say, this is what she thinks of Elana she is a wash board and she loves to make fun of her she is the only fun that she has here, and there is a deal on the table for her to go home with out any one getting hurt."

Now this was good but this is a bit too good she possibly could have heard Scarlet say that some were. "Ok this is for my lawyer and well, 'what aren't you telling us?'"

He grinned at me this was getting weird I think that he may have a crush on me but I had to act like I had no idea what he was talking about. "My client says that she has told you everything and has kept no secrets from . . ."

"That is none of your authority to know."

He sighed "I would beg to differ this is something that I think any one who is held hostage should know what and by whom they are taken by."

He was right "alright you may know this much, we are with the government."

He smiled I was dumbfounded "well I think that there is more that you can tell me agent Adoms."

I sighed he was good and he had a legal back-story. "You got me we are from well what people think that its not there so we are from area 51."

He grinned as if he had won a gold medal in the Olympics. "You are good for this thing that we are going threw . . ."

Then he cut me off "we need to know how we can go from being lawyers back to kids."

That took me off guard this wasn't what I would expect so that question was the thing that caught me off guard. "All that you have to do is crawl out of the ceiling in the bathroom girls but you can use the boys but it's not that easy to maneuver and all that you have to do is ask to go to the bathroom and you are set free."

I said that without thinking I felt like I was the only one that was stressed this time it was just I can't explain the feeling but we had to get back to the principals office. "Ok everyone this is going to be our greatest battle ever this is going to do world war III this is going to be a great we will be famous someday if any one but us knows us or if any one is going to believe us but we will know that this is our school and these are our friends and this is what we can do to prove that this is a battle that no one or some one that knows about this. Are you with me?!"

They all screamed there agreements "got to go."

And we all left the lunchroom and in two minutes we were in the principals' office. We all took a well-deserved rest.

Jason

We slept till noon and I was surprised that they let us sleep that long considering that school was going on like normal. But they locked us in the principal's office so that was a no brainier that we couldn't go anywhere. They were all asleep and I could tell that Scarlet was dreaming that this day was just a dream. Erik was well dreaming about being in project runway and winning. That was normal of him, Zach was dreaming about . . . I can't quite tell but he seams that he's having a good dream about something. Elana was dreaming about how she was going to run the whole school and trying to figure out what will happen. This was a great time for me to try and figure out   what agent Adoms was thinking and if he figured out what we are doing. I couldn't see anyone but the students none of them were looking this way that is when I realized that there was a dark tinted and sound proof window on the thing no one could see us or hear us this was no good.

Elana

My eyes popped open at the slightest touch. When I looked up it was Jason "let me sleep it's in the middle of the night."

I groaned as I rolled over. "Get up it's about one pm!"

My eyes popped out of my sockets "why didn't you wake me up earlier?"

He smiled, "hey don't pin this on me I woke up about three minutes ago." "Wow, I didn't know that being in charge would take so much out of me."

We sat there silently "why haven't you gotten out?"

"The door's locked."

He said apologetically "ok this is going to be easy all I need is one of Scarlet's bobby pins and we are home free."

It took me about three seconds to get out and when we did the whole school was staring at me. "What?"

I asked one of the braver ones looked both ways and then asked, "Why are you kinda glowing purple?"

I looked down and saw what they meant this was my worst nightmare. "Oh it's just the fluorescents, since you never look at me in the halls you wouldn't even know."

That was hard lying to them. "Ok guys this is our only chance to do this if we mess up then that's it were over. We need to get this right the first time, techs do you have my phone, I need it so that it shows that I have had it the whole time."

The one that lead the group handed it to me. "Thanks so much guys."

I smiled gratefully, "now just act like none of this just happened,"

Then one of the kids asked "how did you get out of there we heard that it was locked."

I sighed this was going to be something that isn't good "well I learned that from my sister she is on the Americas most wanted, I cant give away any more information."

They all gasped as if that was something new. "Guys get to class and lock the door I just had to make sure that you all knew the drill."

When we were in there my lawyer um, what was his name Brad locked the door and winked at me I blushed. I turned to Jason and we sat there and talked the whole time when agent Adoms came in we shut it immediately "ok what do you want know you kept us locked in here and for what?"

He seemed to have forgotten that I have a voice inside me and know its coming out. "Um, well do you want lawyers for this questioning?"

He asked "yes and can we use our phones our parents know the lawyers so we will all want to use our phones at   least we would prefer it."

He nodded, "and you can't hack into our phones or I will sue your company for all they've got."

Again he nodded this was getting weird he never agreed to any of my threats. "Well guys we need to get to the bathrooms they have the greatest reception."

Everyone stood up and went for the door we all went to the girls' room and the boys didn't even complain. This was just about break for the first hour and every one was on the phones so just the few other people wouldn't make a difference. I called Brad and said that this was time and so did the rest of them it was going to be the best day in the history of the earth and of kids. "Tell everyone of the groups that are going to do something like the pranksters get them to get there bombs and get the techs to get there knock out gas and just everyone else to get what ever they've got."

This was going to be the time of our lives. "We've got our lawyers and all we need to do is wait for them to be let out for the after lunch walk around."

We all nodded I really had to go to the bathroom "boys why are you here sometimes a girl has to go to, so please leave."

They bolted out of that room as if that was there first plan. We just stood there and looked where they were a smoke shadow was left of them. We laughed then when we were done there we went to the doors and there they were they looked amazing like lawyers were supposed to suite cases monkey suites just every thing that they would need they had. We walked to our assigned lawyers and then we walked back to the principals' office and then we were asked separately what we weren't telling them. This was going to be a blast. Well let's just wait and see.

Scarlet

I was the first one that was going to be questioned. I think that Elana gave me the girl so that the boy didn't get distracted. We sat down in the same seat that I sat in last time and this time no acting like I had no thought in my head, just plain act like myself. "Ok I just need to ask your client a few minor questions is that ok with you and your client?"

I whispered, "Just say that it is fine."

She cleared her throat "my client would like to express all and any of her answers threw me. Is that ok agent . . ."

"Adoms please just call me Adoms."

She smiled "I would rather call you agent Adoms if you may, just call me Kim."

That got his attention "alright Kim where did you go to school to be a lawyer?"

She was grinning "well, I went to Stanford law school it is a very big school but I got around alright."

She batted her eyelashes. Ah, I get it now she flirting with him so that he will let us go easier.

She was good at this, "well is there anything that you would like to discuss with me?"

She asked in her business voice. "Yes I would what does your client think about this girl Elana?"

I whispered, "Just tell him that I like to um make fun of her that she is an easy target or something just make it good."

She nodded and she said this "well this is what my client thinks of her as just an easy target to pick on that she is the only fun that she has in this fun sucked school."

This was good but I think that I've heard that before, he said this after words, "well that is all that I need to know for know, Kim how can I get a hold of you?"

"Oh all that you need to do is call my cell 1586-555-4522, call me at any time."

She winked and flourished out of that room like she was a natural and, she was.

Erik

While I was waiting for Scarlet to come back I was freaking out this is going to horrible, I can't fight any one and if he asks me to tell him about Elana or any of the others I don't think that I can hold back my temper. This is going to be the most difficult thing; they got me a 'lawyer' that can calm me. But I want to get all my anger out on that one little piece of scum. Ok just keep calm just tell my lawyer to do a good job and that he can do it. The tension is killing me. I can't stand being in the room it feels like the walls are closing in. that's when Scarlet's lawyer walked out with Scarlet trailing behind her. Asking her a lot of questions that could have me gagging on the floor. The lady called my name and said "he will be here shortly he just had to call some one for an emergency, or at least that's what he told me."

She led us into the room that he took us in the first day that this happened it feels like we've been here for about three days and I mean that one day trapped in school feels like a few weeks or worse months. "Ok this is what we are here for, he's going to ask about your friends and I need you to stay calm is that going to be a problem?"

I sat there silently to think about that I whispered "yes,"

He sighed this is going   to be the hardest time of his life. "What are you going to do?"

I smiled "you don't want to know."

This is going to be good if he doesn't stop me he probably will though. Here he comes the 'big' man himself. He was and is the worst person that I have met and, I have met Elana's dad and trust me he isn't this heartless. I sank into my chair and hoped that he wouldn't look at me. "Good the giant is here,"

I growled "ok agent, Mr. . . . ."

"Adoms just call me Adoms."

"How about I just call you agent Adoms it has a good ring to it."

He nodded "and I will call you?"

"Chase an ordinary name for an ordinary guy."

He pursed his lips, "ok this is going to be a tough question for Erik, what do you think that other people think of Elana."

I whispered "say that I don't want to talk to him, and what ever you said about Elana behind her back I won't be listening."

He started "my client wouldn't like to talk to you because of the remark about him being a giant, he thinks and knows that people think of her as a freak and he's her friend not for that reason but she is a vary nice girl she is just, well she's getting her voice."

Agent Adoms sucked in a lot of air and let it out slowly. "Ok Erik this is a question for you, what do you think that Elana would do if she were the ruler of the   school?"

I took a deep breath "well for one thing she wouldn't make separate groups that everyone has to be in she would let any one do and show us what they've got. That is what I think."

I stated then fell silent, "ok that will be all thanks to the giant here he just let me know what she would and wouldn't do."

I was going to murder that guy some time or another. So we just walked out and he didn't regret that giant comment but I am going to show him that I'm no push over. "Ok you got him out alive can I hurt him when the battle starts?"

I'm just asking him to make sure that he says no and if he says yes then he better watch out. "Sure have a blast."

He said as we walked out.

Jason

This wasn't what I expected; Erik didn't beat the crap out of that guy even though I saw that comment about the giant. I'm so glad that none of the girls are blonds or there would be fireworks. All of the dumb blond jokes he can think of the girls would be going nuts clawing the guy and just it's too hard to explain. I was waiting for them to come back when I saw him say something like 'can I hurt him after this?' And well I think that his lawyer said that he could this is going to be fun. I waited and waited for them to come up but, they were taking such a long time that I nearly fell asleep. Someone roughly shook me   out of my sleep it was the lady and she said this "its your turn oh what ever you do don't fall asleep. He will tell me that I have to well almost kill you so just try no to."

She winked; this is going to be good. I walked beside my lawyer and started to chew on my thumb. I am going to be the only one who has to talk I had no reason not to, I tried to swallow the lump that was stuck in my throat but, it wouldn't go down. That's when I started to take deep and trying but not too calming. We walked in and then he walked in with a big grin on his face like some one spilt the secret. Oh I've heard Elana talk about this it is just one of those things that get you to think that the other one told him the secret, so that I would spill the beans. This wasn't going to work I knew all his strategies. He had nothing on me. And I was glad about that, but he was still looking as if he heard some thing from a little bird, well that's just what he is going to say about that. "Ok, this is going to be a blast, a little birdie told me about your secret and well you may think that you may be able to do this but no you cant I know everything that you have done and I'm on to all of you."

He sat down and put his fingertips together and just watched I asked my lawyer "what am I going to say?"

"Well all that you have to do is ask what are we doing and then he will have nothing to say, if he dose then we are busted."

I cleared my throat and said "well if you know what we are doing then what are we doing if you answer correctly then I will tell you and if you are incorrect then I will tell you that you are incorrect nothing more nothing less, agreed?"

I asked, he smirked yea I know how to play the game to bozo. He had to think about that if his little charade was going to be flushed down the toilet. "Well, what they told me is that you are going to try and get out,"

I smiled this is good but that was so wrong. "Sorry sir that is so wrong, I don't think that you have the guts to realize what is going to happen, just think about that."

He looked as if that was one of the nuclear bomb had gone off his pants, and I mean that would have been so funny. My lawyer spoke up for the first time, "well if you aren't going to charge my client for anything then we can go is that correct?"

He looked rejected "yes you may,"

then he looked defeated this is going to be amazing he isn't going to know anything. We walked triumphantly out of that place. I was so happy that I jumped for joy in the   hallway.

Zach

I was talking with my lawyer and we were laughing about all the pranks that we've played on the teachers. When we saw that Jason was jumping on his way out of the principals' office, he was the only one that had to talk and I'm guessing that agent Adoms did that little birdie bit, and man did he get it wrong by the way Jason is jumping he got it so wrong that it is laughable. "Yo, dude what happened in there?"

I said as I high-five him, "I think that you know what happened, I can tell that you know this,"

Aw man I hate him for that but I want to know what happened in there. "Alright you got me there, but what did he say that we are going to do?"

"He said that we were going to find a way to run away from this joint."

We all laughed that was so wrong, well the lady came and grabbed my by the shoulder and dragged me to the room. This was not cool this is harassment; I could call the cops on these creeps any time that I want. But our plan is going to be much more fun. I cant wait till Elana gets her interrogation over with and we get to go back to our 'normal' day and when she says we get to go, first the pranksters would set off there bombs and then we would all go in and get them all to show us where they are from. This plan is practically fool proof, but if one of our people were to go to the dark side. But we were already in the principals' office. I sat down cautiously. The room was darker then I remember, but that wasn't going to happen unless he promised them that they could get out. But that was slim to none, while I was getting board out of my mind he walked in and just started with no notification that we there, "ok this will be easier if you would just let me explain, don't just jump in when ever you think that I'm wrong, here we go I know what you guys are up to but don't get me wrong it's a spot on plan but you see I don't think kids like you are going to stand up against us then you have a lot on   your plate son,"

I smirked at him he's not going to make me say anything. "Ok um, first you have that so wrong all we want to do is go home is there a problem with that?"

He shook his head like he just couldn't believe that we wanted out this is a shocker, "well do you have anything to say to my client or if you would like to charge him with something then go ahead but if not then we should be able to leave, is that correct?"

He nodded to the door. "You may leave now."

We walked out of there like there was no tomorrow; we both were exhausted and well just so shaken up.

Elana

This isn't good everyone went besides me; I bet that he's saving his best for last or should I say the worst of his schemes. The girl came out and she was sweating threw all her clothes, "ok you want us to come?"

She smiled apologetically "yes if you would please this is getting even more stressful every time that I do this, so if you could just go and be good for him. If you could tell him everything that you know so that we don't have to stay here any longer, one of our guards had a spaz attack, so just be a good girl so that we all can get out of here. Please I'm begging you."

I chewed on my bottom lip and thought that over "Ill tell him all that I can with giving all names; oh and that includes you so do you want me to tell him something or nothing?"

Her eyes looked like they were about to pop out of their sockets "just tell him nothing, and I will never sign up for this job again alright kid lie like there is no tomorrow?"

I smiled "will do."

As we left my lawyer smiled and I just laughed he was so hitting on me but that was no biggie I was getting used to it and well it was just getting plain annoying. "Ok I've had enough! Stop flirting with me this is insane!"

He looked taken aback, "I thought at first that it was cute but now it's just out of control you need to act like an adult in there and if you even try to flirt with me one more time I swear that I   will get you! Do you get me?"

I looked him strait in the eye he stopped smiling immediately and nodded solemnly and started to act mature as if I just said the magical word that got any guy to shut it and act as old as you are. When we got in there we acted as if the hallway was a year and a half ago "thank you for coming Elana, and . . ."

Brad cleared his throat "Brad just call me Brad and I will call you agent Adoms, or at least that is what my client told me to call you,"

"And that is fine, I will just plead with your client, please just tell me something I will do anything for a single word from you,"

I had a sly smile on my face "alright you get your wish,"

Brad looked as though I said that there was a nuclear bomb going off when I whispered "my little bro taught me this one," I winked "come here, closer, closer, closer."

Then I burped in his ear as loud as I could and Brad was smiling and I looked agent Adoms in the face and said "was that good enough for you?"

But he was still in shock and I just waited for him to come back to our world "what was that?"

He asked flabbergasted "oh that was just me, can we go I have a lot more then that, so are you going to do some thing or do we just walk out?"

His hand motioned to the door, when we got out we high-five each other and he started laughing "that was the best thing in the world I don't think that any one did that except you, I'm so proud of you." He came in for the hug "No, no, no. What did I say in the just a few minuets ago?" he retreated immediately I pat him on the head "that's better," and we were out of that black hole. We were still laughing when we got into the to office's waiting room and high-fived everyone that I could "guys don't you know that whole burping thing where you tell someone to come closer and then burp right into agent Adoms ear and I think that he is having a smell attack right at this vary moment." We all just started laughing and then we just walked out of the door and into the normal school day.

Agent Adoms

This is getting weird they normally just fight with me not burp my ear off. But she had good intentions with that one word thing; she didn't say one word that was a good thing or she would have told me that I had to leave her and her friends alone. So that wouldn't be vary good but they did get there laugh I think I even saw the lawyer smirk just a bit or that could just have just been my imagination. "I really need to pull my self together."

I told my self.

Elana

As always I was walking with Erik and Jason while every one was eyeing me in the halls, with a small nod that told them that the plan was still on. Then they went to pass the message to anyone that had said yes to the thing. But the biggest problem was that the teachers were giving me the stink   eye. Even the teachers that had sympathy for me, the only one that didn't do that to me was Mr. Gringer he smiled at me warmly as if this whole thing was just a dream, but he was asking me with his eyes if I had a plan on the inside that I let none of the teachers or adults know and I kinda nodded. And he seemed sort of satisfied about that I could come up with a plan like that and with a voice to I think that he was the only teacher that is proud that I have a voice and I'm letting it out. But we were close to lunch and that is when our plan is going to go out. I walked to the nerds and asked well I kinda whispered, "Do you have that K O spray with you? If you do then bring it to lunch."

They all nodded and showed me the canisters, I grinned they are doing there part. So all that I had to do is ask the pranksters if they were ready for the war that lies ahead, but they are ready for going to juvie. Here it goes were in Chemistry and we are working with chemicals so this was a time that the prank leader can have some time for more stink bombs, and I will get an A+ for what I'm going to write the patriotic table and label what they all are used for like so: Hydrogen, Lithium, Beryllium, est. Hydrogen uses: Rocket Fuel, Welding, and filling balloons. And so on. But this was a perfect time for me just to relax and think about what may happen next. Well the teacher came up behind me *this is going to be another one of those how could you do this to the school acts.* I thought but she had something else to say to me "you know that you are the only person to do the patriotic table? I would say that you have the easy A."

She winked as she walked away. That wasn't what I expected but she was trying to be nice to me after what happened at the school yesterday, the bell rung and it was lunch guards at every door and well just about every exit. We are going to play telephone I whispered "were going to start with the nerds and they need to spray then go for the whole place to be ours   and were free. Pass that on," when it was half way across the room all the nerds stood up and each one went to one of the guards, I put my hand where they could see it but not the guards then counted down 5, 4, 3, 2, 1, 0. Then you heard the soft hissing of an aerosol can, going, going, going, gone. They were out cold I stood up and yelled, "Are you ready for this?"

They all yelled there response, "we are kids, not animals that can be kept in a cage! We can do any thing if we put our minds to it are we going to let them treat us like were just thing that add a complication?"

Angry kids were yelling "no!"

And the rest were yelling that to, "here we come government and we aren't happy! Get what you have and we are going out there to fight for what we believe in!"

everyone rushed to get what they had from there back packs and man did these people know how to save space in there back packs, it was like they all had *Marry Poppins* Magic bag that could fit a whole person in it. Half the boys had there b-b guns or paint ball guns, the girls got the nerds to make them a lipstick that is a very sticky situation if you get her to push the button. All that I had were about a hundred angry kids that want to go home and will kill for that freedom and to get to go where these people work or we will hand them over to the well lets just say that there are collage kids that have anger issues and well will let us live if they get to beat up an adult, that had me smiling deviously. We all knew the school and what are the best hiding places so that no one will know where we are. But there are some complications like where we can't go no matter what those places are the teachers' lounge and the parking lot or the front door. I looked out the door and listened for any boots or silent footsteps; there was nothing that I could hear. So I motioned for them to come and we were going to have the most of one day, we had to be very quiet so that they couldn't find us or know what we are doing. There was a gape in the silence and I heard combat boots five feet and closing bathroom on the right Chemistry lab to the left, I nudged Jason "chem. Lab or bathroom?"

He nodded to the chem. Lab I opened the door and said "get in there"

They all did what I said. But they all quieted as soon as they entered the room I whispered "what is it?"

I looked and saw that there were guards everywhere and they had all the kids in there grasps two to a person and then I heard agent Adoms coming this way and there were no more guards to hold me down so, I slid a note that I made if this happened into Jason's hand with out the guards seeing it or feeling it. I sprinted out of that room there was nothing that they could do so I went in to the bathroom and in the ceiling. I heard agent Adoms come in then walk out but he did leave one of his guards there to make sure that I didn't escape, if he thought I was there at all or had someone told him about the ceiling? Either way this is bad   they knew what we are up to but hey, they don't know me know that I have learned about friend ship and that you can't leave a man behind no matter what.

Jason

I watched her sprint out of the room. The note was still in my hand, Agent Adoms was asking us where she went. To be totally honest I had no clue where she was going or how she as going to get us out. After Agent Adoms left I was hog tied and duck tape across my mouth, this is when I looked at the note. It read:

I have not had a better friend then you. I will possibly be in the ceiling by the time you read this. But I have to go alien there is no other way to get to my parents. If you or any of the others are harmed I will take it as my own pain. This may be good-bye for a long time. But I would like to say this; I love you, I will never stop loving you. If you don't feel the same I understand. But know this you where always here for a certain reason don't forget that. My parents are the world to me, that recording is for you. I will get both if I can, but it I don't I'm so sorry. This is good bye for now, I hope.

Elana

One tear escapes my eye. I say the words that I've wanted to tell her ever since I met her in my head, *I love you.* Then they take me into a corner of the room, and started to ask me questions I had no answer for. So when I didn't answer I got punched, then I hear a voice echo off of the walls.

Elana

They are getting on my nerves and trust me that is no were some one would like to be, so I found where they are keeping them and man did they mean business they had them hog tied, that just got me mad they had Jason all alone and we questioning him about me and they were hitting him and every one else and man did they have a lot of explaining to do when I got to them, the guards came back and said that they couldn't find me, they said that I must have fled the school. I laughed at that in my head, *yea right I would never do that to any one.* I thought and then there was agent Adoms he had someone with him that I guessed was a bad thing then he asked the question that was my quoi to go down and beat the heck out of those people first with a flick of my wrist all the weapons flew out of every ones hand and I mad my voice sound like it was from a horror movie "this is what happens when you get me mad!"

and I sank down and I had complete hatred for him and the rest of his goons I lifted my arms and sent a gust of wind and had them all pined against the back wall I walked over there and they all just had there mouths hanging open, palms up I had everything levitating except my friends "well this is where you ask what I am,"

They were all to shocked to answer that so I did "I'm the one that you are looking for and yea I want my parents and yea I'm an alien so just get with the program."

I winked I flicked my wrist one more time and I flooded the room but I had air bubbles around my friends mouths I put my hands down, "are you going to take us there or not if not then you will see me in a way that no one wants to see so, yes or no?" agent Adoms piped up "No never," I smiled "alright then I will have to get my friends and well lets see what you think when you see me." I snapped   my fingers and there were snakes coiling around each one of them, "oh if you squirm they will get tighter and well you get the rest." I levitated my friends out of the room and untied Jason and he got to work with the others "ok who was dumb enough to squirm while I was gone?"

All of them did and they all were turning red "what did I tell you?"

I snapped and the snakes disappeared and well I turned into what I really am a purple phantom with a green tinge I zapped them not to hard but enough to shock them enough so that they would talk "Ok I am going to ask this one more time, take us to area 51 or I will kill you alright? When do we leave?"

One of the guards edged agent Adoms to say yes this is all that came out of agent Adoms "tomorrow eight am sharp if you are late . . ." "If we are late   you will wait for us or you will die and I will get my parents out of there myself and tell General Peaters that you gave me the ok to be there."

I changed back to my normal self and walked out everyone was untied "ok guys we have to be up at eight sharp got that they are taking us to area 51 so I can see my parents and so that Jason here can meet the real Einstein you know that they have him preserved there, and that should be a good thing for you the only existing reincarnation of Einstein himself and well I think that you may be able to fly the jet out of here if they decide to bail right?"

He nodded and I think I saw just a hint of redness in his neck that is one reason that I lov- like him, but I'll let that slide while the questions came on me like a waterfall 'what is your home planet?' 'How come didn't you get caught by area 51 guards?' and well I just zoned in on something else that I was hearing foot steps and they are from tennis shoes and well I know the only teacher in the school that wears those "Mr. Gringer,"

I said out loud they all turned and saw that he was coming down the hall, "that was vary brave of you princess,"

He said I nodded and curtsied "yes but I did what had to be done, unless you want the king and queen stuck in there for the rest of there lives. Witch let me remind you is just about forever on this planet, well you know they can't die here, even if they wanted to."

I looked at him with sad eyes then he hugged me "thank you night I will forever owe thee,"

Then I looked back at them I sighed "yes I'm the princess on my home planet, but I like life here much better thank you vary much. The only thing that is missing is my parents and dude I want them so badly, so we have to get them please I'm just asking as a friend, not an up tight princess so, if you could come with me,"

I put my hand in the middle and the rest piled there's on top "we have got this far I say that we go all the way"

"Alright 1, 2, 3, all the way! Were going tomorrow and there is nothing that can stop us from saving my parents. We've got a long day a head of us, so we better get cracken'"

So we went on with our normal day and well when that day ended we went into the office and fell asleep for the rest of the day, then my watch went off at 7 and I got everyone up and got them all to the bathrooms, man do I feel like a mother, "guys brush your teeth, I don't care if you don't have a tooth brush just use your finger."

When we got out everyone looked as if they just came from their house. "Ok guys we have about fifteen minutes to kill so lets go over what we want from area 51, for instance I want my parents back, Scarlet?"

She thought about what she could have from area 51 that she could possibly want, "pictures of different colors that aren't known to man or woman."

I nodded thoughtfully "Jason?"

His was the easiest "I want to hear Einstein so that I can ask why I was made a reincarnation of himself in me."

I smiled "Zach?"

He smiled "the smelliest thing that they have and to know how to make more."

I giggled he was going to get the best thing more stink bombs and man will they stink. "Well we only have ten minutes and we need to find them if they bailed I will get the snakes to find them and squeeze the last drop of life out of there soulless life, sorry I just am so mad at them."

They all started laughing, "Ok Elana, that is not something that I would hear from a princess,"

Now I understood why they were all laughing I smiled "ok they are almost here five feet and closing."

There they were just walking as calm as ever. "Ok where is the plane, helicopter? What ever it is that we are going to take to go to area 51 to get my parents and well a little something else for everyone else and we will leave there peacefully unless you make me get mad again and we all don't want that; let's go."

They all looked so scared agent Adoms "but we need you to turn all of your friends invisible so that you can get everything that you desire and we all will act like all this never happened."

We all exchanged a few looks that helped us decide if we would do that "alright but we get what we want and no one gets hurt got that?"

They all nodded nervously and we all grabbed hands and I turned us all invisible so that they couldn't see us at all. "Ok we can't make a noise until we are on area 51 soil and we can see my parents, k?"

They all nodded but they were all looking at a vary tall guy with a buzz cut and shades just like agent Adoms and he had crystal clear blue eyes under those shades. They talked and well he motioned us to come with him but the general thought that he was motioning for the guards to come. But this was about a five-minuet ride to the area but we were playing rock paper scissors muted version. It was so fun we hit the ground with a lot of force that I almost lost the connection that kept us invisible; this was going to be the most fun that I've had all this time on earth. We are off that stuffy thing when we got out we all stretched my muscles are so stiff, and I think that the rest of them felt that way to. We are just three feet from the jail cell that they have my parents in I can just feel it. Agent Adoms was talking to the guy with the buzz cut and glasses, saying that they had to move the aliens because there were people that knew where there. He was doing well for someone that was being forced to do it. "Alright if it is fine with you I'll get my guys to get them out with out any hassle, it that is ok with you sir,"

As we walked through the doors it was just one big room made of mostly stainless steal. Shelves of different chemicals and body parts I saw a pair of eyes. I shivered. This was just getting to weird for me. There was a wall of Plexiglas that held my parents and I saw video cameras all around. The fluorescents' where so white that I saw the dust partials floating in the air. While walking I saw everything from the planets, some type of plant, or rocks from that planet. It was all so strange to me I only knew of people going to Mars and the Moon. Not, Jupiter, Saturn, or Uranus. How did they get there? But there is a time for questions and a time for answers. The time for answers was now.

The buzz cut guy nodded and left with all of his burly guards. I rolled my eyes as they talked about my parents always giving a hassle. They wouldn't hurt a fly, but they had their breakdowns when I wasn't there, what can I say they are parents that have their flaws like everyone else. He said, "Ok guys Elana get your parents and well what dose the others want?"

Jason smiled and said, "I want to hear that recording that Einstein recorded, I want to know why I live with his memories."

Agent Adoms nodded to an old recording device, and Jason went there when he saw that he nodded to it, Scarlet was up next and this is what she spoke for the first time "I want to see some colors that aren't known to anyone outside of this office so that I can make well you know what why should I tell you but if you could that would be great,"

I saw that he had to think about that so then I went to the nastiest request "Zach,"

His face lit up like a Christmas tree. "I want the smelliest thing that you have and I want to know how to make it."

Agent Adoms grabbed a tube and just gave us a whiff and I was about to keel over, it smelled like bad breath, skunk spray, rotting meat, and swamp water. All combined and I don't think that is a good idea to let him have that, but that is what he really wants. "We haven't came up with a name for it but I think this is what you want and how to create this is you have to get all the things that you smell in this and what you think that you should add, and well put it in an air tight container and well the rest is vary complicated."

But Zach knew what he had to do, and well kids better run when they see him with a stink bomb or they are in for a blast of stinks of all types. "Well that's everyone and where are my parents?"

He pointed to a cage that is lined with that plastic glass stuff that is unbreakable, or that's what they think for humans of course we aliens have a lot of powers that you humans can't use but you do have. My parents could've got out of there easily but they possibly were too afraid that it would give away where I was. I knocked on the glass and they looked up and smiled broadly when I pressed the button I ran in their hugged them and whispered, "I love you,"

They were crying but they are tears of happiness. They were in their alien state and then they both went into there human state and they both looked just like me, same color eyes and hair but they had a different skin complexion they were tanner then me I was an albino in both planets (go figure), that is were they found out that I had powers that none of the other aliens had, that's why I had to be home schooled, the alien government was about to execute me when they heard that I was more powerful then the president himself and that is how they chose the leader or president as they called it here. "Mom, Dad, we need to stay here so that I can live family, and I need my stuff and so do you. Mom I think that you could get a job as a five star chef and trust me you can, there is one in this place that has had the sign up for a few weeks and I don't think that they have found someone that has as much talent as you do mom. Dad you could be an um? Dad I don't think that you have told me what you are good at, so what are you good at?"

He smiled and said in his velvety voice "I love to be with children and well, remember while we were on our planet I was a teacher for the third graders."

I nodded he was amazing with kids I had the perfect job for him "dad you should go back to what you love doing being with children go back to being a teacher in this world."

They both nodded and I had my family back together. Everyone looked to me then to my parents they all asked, "These are your parents?"

I smiled and looked to them and back to my friends "yea, yea they are."

They both had there hands on my shoulders and looking at my friends "Oh mom dad this is Jason, Zach, Scarlet, and Erik the ones who helped me threw this whole thing."

Agent Adoms

I can't believe my eyes this girl actually has done what many people have only attempted. I actually feel pride in this girl. I walk over to her and solute her. She does the same. "Good job. I would give you a medal but that won't be necessary would it?"

She smiles and shakes her head. "No but thanks for the offer."

I smile and say, "You have succeeded in what many have only attempted. And I am shocked and proud of you. You kept your friends in front of your own. I don't have half of the neck that you do. Yesterday, if someone would to have told me that a seventeen year old was going to invade Area 51 I would have thought them crazy. But you have proved them all wrong. And I solute you for that."

I solute again and walk out of the room for a few brief words with General Peaters. He was astounded by my story and wanted to meet Elana. But I made him swear on the bible that he wouldn't do anything to her. We walk into the room. Elana has a glaring contest with General

Peaters. I break the silence. "So General is there anything you would like to tell Elana?"

He grunts and nods. "I would like to thank you for this little game and I solute you. You have done a good job, little thief. You where the first one that I couldn't crack."

He paused for a second possibly because he was yelling the whole time. "But you where also the one that. I have been looking for, for about five years. That is a big record with me and well I guess that you can get away with another twenty years. I think that we all deserve a break after this, but what do you say that we do this next year?"

He all but yelled with a wink and she blushed. "I don't have school next year this is my Senior year and I don't think that I will be making a habit of this anyways." And we smile and walk away but then the Mr. what's-his-face walks up to us and places one finger on our foreheads and we both black out.

This looked like a perfect family picture with my best friends with me. I heard Mr. Gringer coming down the hall "you did well princess, and I well erased everyone's mind from what happened, is that alright princess?"

I nodded "could you stop calling me princess, only call me princess on our planet, on this one just call me Elana."

He looked offended "ok pri- Elana, are these ones good with what happened today?"

I looked at Scarlet she rolled her eyes "yea you can trust me, I would love to be friends with you if that is ok with you I don't want people looking up to me like I'm the big cheese, I would like to be just another student."

I smiled that was the nicest thing that she has said all this time that we have been stuck together "and I say that you can just stop stapling things to your self just be your self be comfortable in your own skin like I am, k?"

She nodded like she's been wanting for some one to say that for years. "Yea, Gringer they all are fine,"

I waited for agent Adoms to say something, "Oh Mr. Adoms we need our stuff if you please."

Then I whispered to Gringer "erase his memory to, I don't want him to tell any one about what has happened the last few days."

He nodded and halfway bowed and I gave him the not on this planet stare, he stopped and walked away and I walked to my parents UFO and got out all that we had in there. As we got into it and I turned it into a yellow Camaro with two green pinstripes, I always have wanted that car so that's what I turned our UFO into. So we just drove out of their, my friends and I had to squeeze into the back, but we all love the car it. I grabbed a string that was just sitting in my lap and we all played a lot of games of cat cradle and we all showed each other what we could do in the world of cat cradle and I did the hand trick where they put there hand in and there hand is stuck in the string and then when they put there hand threw again and it was out Scarlet did the witches broom, Zach did cats whiskers, Jason did the Navajo Jump, and Erik did the cup and saucer and then into the Eiffel tower. We had a lot of fun and it was a good thing that they knew how to drive this thing. Then we were at my house and the parents were all an illusion I just made them up even my sister that is on Americas Most Wanted, all that was just my imagination. "Guys I think that the bus is going to be coming any second now and no one will remember anything not even the battle the lawyers wont remember what they did no one will remember us."

I looked to my parents while my throat burned and my eyes were going to start watering but I blinked that thought away from mind. "This was a good day for us and everyone that helped but won't remember, let's go inside and get something to eat this was a day that we will never forget, and I just want to say that it was the most fun that I've had my whole time that I've been here."

We all went into the house and it was all changed so that my parents could get there jobs there were collage degrees on one wall that said my dad was qualified for a teaching job, and that my mom is able and certified to be a five star chef and this is a life that I will love and cherish for the rest of my life, when they left to act like they came home from school I grabbed a football that was sitting on the table and ran out side with my dad and people were staring at us but I didn't care I was having fun with my real dad. I grabbed it and started running and he grabbed me by my waist and lifted my up in the air and took the football, later my mom came out and said that dinner was ready. I wish that I could freeze this moment so that I could just be happy, but this was a great time I heard the door bell and I got it and saw that it was Jason and I forgot the he was just about three inches above me "hi, Jason what do you want?"

I asked he whispered, "I have to do this,"

He leaned down and kissed me, my hands tangled in his hair and his hands were around my waist. We pulled apart I said, "I thought that you would never do that."

And I kissed him lightly on the lips, "see you at school tomorrow."

He smiled and said "yea see you tomorrow."

Then he winked and left, I went back to my parents, later after high school and a few years of collage, I finally said yes to marring Jason after my parents said that it was fine and after all this my parents and I were never bothered by any one from our planet or yours.

Epilogue

"Jason?" He looks up from the news paper, "yes?" I smiled. "What did the recording say? I've always wondered thinking that you where going to tell me but you never did." He returned the smile. "It said that I was going to change the world and enjoy it." I smiled "are you enjoying it?" He smiled and said, "When I'm with you I will always enjoy it." And he kissed me. The rest is a mystery but is still being written. But the next part wont be in you next history class.